T0303733

More Praise for
By the Lemon Tree

"There is no single ideal of American fiction, but there are books that capture the many essences of this country—the geography of the land, the weather, the layers of civilization and punishment and possibility and loss that rests over and under all of our cities and small towns, the ways in which the past is always coming upon us and why the future is both a confusion and a romance. In *By the Lemon Tree*, Keenan Norris crafts stories that hold these essences in each sentence and scene and we find our self in central California, hot and wild, and funny and tragic and captivated in a way only the best stories can. *By the Lemon Tree* gives the reader an intimate and immediate connection to the African American experience in central California, the child's experience in the land of adults, the lovelorn in the land of cynics, and these are experiences that will linger with readers long after these stories come together and go apart."

– **LALEH KHADIVI**, *A Good Country*

By the Lemon Tree

Keenan Norris

NOMADIC PRESS

OAKLAND

111 FAIRMOUNT AVENUE
OAKLAND, CA 94611

BROOKLYN

475 KENT AVENUE #302
BROOKLYN, NY 11249

WWW.NOMADICPRESS.ORG

MASTHEAD

FOUNDING AND MANAGING EDITOR
J. K. FOWLER

ASSOCIATE EDITOR
MICHAELA MULLIN

EDITING AND DESIGN
J. K. FOWLER

MISSION STATEMENT

Nomadic Press is a 501 (C)(3) not-for-profit organization that supports the works of emerging and established writers and artists. Through publications (including translations) and performances, Nomadic Press aims to build community among artists and across disciplines.

SUBMISSIONS

Nomadic Press wholeheartedly accepts unsolicited book manuscripts. To submit your work, please visit www.nomadicpress.org/submissions

DISTRIBUTION

Orders by trade bookstores and wholesalers:
Small Press Distribution,
1341 Seventh Street
Berkeley, CA 94701
spd@spdbooks.org
(510) 524-1668 / (800) 869-7553

By the Lemon Tree

© 2018 by Keenan Norris

This book was made possible by a loving community of chosen family and friends, old and new.

For author questions or to book a reading at your bookstore, university/school, or alternative establishment, please send an email to info@nomadicpress.org.

Cover and back artwork by Arthur Johnstone

Published by Nomadic Press, 111 Fairmount Avenue, Oakland, CA 94611

Third printing, 2021

LIBRARY OF CONGRESS CATALOGING-IN-PUBLICATION DATA

Norris, Keenan, 1981 –
Title: *By the Lemon Tree*
P. CM.
Summary: Set in the Central California countryside and the Southern California desert, *By the Lemon Tree*'s old school stories chronicle the collision of wide-eyed childhood with the end of lives, human and animal. In "Twice Good," a downtrodden city administrator shows up for a Black Panther protest forty years too late. "Funeral in Fresno" introduces us to an impatient reverend who is forced to confront his past and his future, while in the title story, a young boy born and raised in East Oakland bears witness to life and death in an ancient rural world.

[1. FICTION. 2. AFRICAN AMERICAN. 3. CALIFORNIA. 4. AMERICAN GENERAL.] I. III. TITLE.

2018958530

ISBN: 978-1-7323340-6-9

By the Lemon Tree

Keenan Norris

**NOMADIC
PRESS**

CONTENTS

TWICE GOOD

Subject: The End
Time: 3:00AM
From: Vincent Cameron Deveraux
To: drcasey@reagan.org; mgraziano@cityofsansuerte.com; ppauludny@
cityofsansuerte.com; revsherwood@cityofsansuerte.com; marguello@
cityofsansuerte.com; raquel.jiminez@cityofsansuerte.com; kaseem.james@csusb.
edu; vrodriguez@csusb.edu; ogwumike.ownershipgroup@gmail.com

Hello, everybody,

After close consideration, I've come to the conclusion that the river walk is not
feasible. Though it is a project we have worked toward for some time now, it is
my conclusion that the competing interests of capital, labor, and community are
simply irreconcilable. Each of these class and political positions is in itself valid,
but when brought into alliance, they are prohibitive of one another and, in such
a large-scale context as the construction of a downtown river walk that's cost is
estimated in the millions, they cannot cohere.

We are an apartheid collective, divided along all-too familiar and intractable lines
of interest, ideology, and power.

I hope that another person independent from election and constituency will step
forward and carry this city's renovation forward—but I am done.

On another note, many of us that are of a certain age and size are not in the best of
health. We've wasted countless hours and much fitness at our meetings; meetings
that have produced little but fertile space for hypertension, heart disease, coronary
disease, heart attack and stroke, diabetes and sexual dysfunction. We are not young
people. It is a concern to consider. Blessings.

– Vincent C. Deveraux

YOUR COLLEAGUES CANNOT COALESCE around a single plan, their
center cannot hold (because there is no center), the blood-dimmed tide of

their do-nothingness has long since been loosed. Yes, you still have those lines in your head. Out of USC some forty years and, still, Yeats, he is as relevant as ever. Your city is slouching to Bethlehem just like his Irish.

You want release, you want catharsis, you want a crime, you want peace. Downstairs, you wrestle your leather jacket and cowboy hat from the thicket of clothes in your walk-in closet. Remember, you were once quite the conservative corporatist, cowboy movie-loving, glad-handing good old boy, so your Stetson hat is white as perceived virtue instead of the Black Panther beret you suddenly wish it was.

In the garage, you take your shotgun which you favor for shooting skeet down from its high shelf behind the surfboard, the croquet set and things. Your low back flares because that's what happens when an old man reaches recklessly. But you ignore it. You assemble the shotgun carefully and quietly even though no one but you is home to hear it. As you bend down to take the shells out of their small box underneath the refrigerator, something strikes hard in your chest. You rub at it a second and it subsides. You are old enough to remember when it was still legal in California to possess a loaded firearm in public as long as it was not concealed and not held in a threatening manner, yet you feel freer and younger than you have in years, and closer to eternity, too. Seize the time, Seale told you those many years ago, before you flipped the script on that style of thought and action. Seize the time.

You do not load the gun but rather place it and the ammunition in the passenger seat of your sports car and rev its engine. It is a dormant beast, this beautiful car. You save it for your dates with Faith and even then, for fear of being the kind of brother who does such things, you never really let it roar. Down from your hills and into Suerte's flat lands, you tug all the sound and speed you can out of her. Seize the time, for real. In the city proper, you notice that all the street lights have been turned off: The city is saving money, as usual. After the darkened length of Seccombe Park, then you come up A and B Street and C and then past the Del Taco at D.

Between E and F, you remember, is where the river walk should have been built years ago, where, if Mayor Jiminez and city councilors Casey and Sherwood and Arguello and Pauludny, could get their shit together something of consequence would now stand. You park beside the DMV and ponder things for a second, the city, its corruption, your only heroes railroaded, dismissed black men like yourself. You do not identify with President Obama; he is too young, too guileless, too much loved. You load the shells. You sling the rifle over your shoulder. Seize the time.

You march your newly openly militant self past the government buildings, DMV, Federal Bank, City Hall, the County rehabilitation center.

Here is the cast iron statue of Cesar Chavez, be-shitted by birds, but proud, resplendent when there is sun. You study the great man's rendering, his hard, metallic lines. This was where the river walk was to begin in the most recently discarded plan. It would go gurgling up after a long passage down from the mountains and up from the underground aqueducts. The courtyard was to be razed and a clear glass walk built above the river's flow. The walk was to be constructed in an easy, gradual dome, sloping down on either side and rising to a height of no more than ten feet at its mid-point. Garden beds of roses would ride either side of the river. It was to be so beautiful.

You march on and you grind your teeth just thinking about all the pettiness, the endless pettiness of city politics, the in-fighting, the secret pacts that ensured that nothing would ever be done, and the arguments over trivia: For example, about the construction of a second statue, there were Shakespearean debates. Your black allies wanted a statue of the mulatto governor Pío Pico because they felt that that was empowering somehow, where you felt it was less than deal-breaking. The tribes called for a Tongva Indian. The Mexicans, who were the majority, wanted everything, but specifically, in that scenario, their great Mariano Guadalupe Vallejo getting shit-faced eternally by the birds. And the whites put in their bids for Ronald Reagan, for John Wayne, for anybody who had stopped short of owning slaves.

A homeless man rises into a half-hunch and stares you over sideways. You are about to tip your John Wayne when the man faints dead away. A shame, you think; motherfucker does too many drugs.

You keep marching.

Further on, at the half-mile mark is the statue of the Virgin; a simple stone figure flecked with dirt and yet more bird shit. There was much debate in meetings about to what to do with her once the walk was built above her and the river ran right through her plot of land. Some wanted to remove her to the top of the walk itself while others sided with keeping her where she was on some sort of cement platform shaded by the walk and surrounded by the waters. You were ready to sculpt Lucifer himself if it would bring some business to town: To seize a moment, any moment, out of the whole rush of your decades, so many passionless protests, to have just a moment of time where you can know of yourself that you are what a brother of a certain age means when he announces he's *good*, which is different than the dismissal that millennials mean by it. For you, it would mean you are full, your exhaustion is earned, all is done; you could die then without fear on that clock hand.

You shrug the rifle off your shoulder. One hand on the barrel, the other on the trigger, you handle it, aim it at the high Clock Tower that rises above the government buildings, sighting center mass in between the numbers where only the seconds are not still. But you have never been the man you have always wished you could be. You have never counted yourself among your heroes.

A police car siren wails out and penetrates the time of your anger. You begin to return to our common world and something in you sets itself in dull durance against delegated suicide. Your mind climbs from the drowning waters, reaches the bank, and leaves the brink. You re-situate the rifle on your shoulder. Yet you have not finished the route of your river walk yet. The long walk above the river was to extend over a mile in length. Again, debate about the river walk's precise length persisted, with some in the business community preferring a smaller, more centralized scape and others in government wanting a grander three mile gesture of a creation that would stretch out of the city center and into the near Westside, where the downtown ends and the thrift shops and barrios resume. In light of this, you might march for hours. You hear the siren again but cannot judge if it is emerging closer or receding into the neighborhoods. You reflect that it was the third member of the Panthers, Aoki, and the NRA itself that betrayed the Panthers' stance on guns: Aoki was a hoodlum with charges pending who turned informant, infiltrating the black militants just to keep his own crooked self out the pen. The NRA supported the repeal of California's open-carry law after Newton and Seale marched with their rifles through the State Capitol.

You come to the state flag on its high pole: It flutters at full-mast above all the downtown government buildings, the tainted statues, the shuttered mall, the clumsy little storefronts. You take inventory of the flag in its parts, grizzly bear, red, green and white embroidery, quite like the

Mexican flag, truth be told, just a different animal or two. And beyond the flag hovers the late, pale death-colored moon and the sun's first flickering, red and pink and yellow spotting the skyline without pattern. It is time to head back.

Returning, you note the day laborers: They post themselves like Xeroxed flyers upon walls and lampposts and scattered along curb sides. They see you, too, and in their unmoved silent regard seem to understand the ancient repealed forgotten law in a way that you are painfully aware but few who were alive to witness its death do, that it is no crime for a man to chart the coordinates of his journey and his loss. They gaze at you steadily, without fear or sympathy or anything but hard eyes that know deeper desperations. You tip your hat to them and you retreat the final blocks to the beautiful beast of an automobile that your years of futile labor have won you. And now, you do not feel better, you do not feel worse.

❧

RETIREMENT PROVES CHALLENGING. WEEKDAYS lose their literality and become symbols. The pensioner knows, by state mandate, that his yesterdays outnumber his tomorrows, that there will be no more satisfaction in data sheets, meeting minutes, end of the year parties. Data, minutes, months, years are meaningless now. Your time is finite; that is what all those numbers now mean. Something other than the old black bromide about being twice as good must apply because you cannot be twice as good at realizing the self. This is no longer a contest. You would just like to be good, in the real sense of that word, for once.

Maybe you are jumping the gun, but you don't care. Either you do something soon, or you will find yourself on the far side of so many blank days that you won't know how to get back to this place where, for better or worse, you had the chance to choose. A couple weeks after your emailed resignation, you make up your mind about the woman in your life. It doesn't take long for you to decide how it will go: Refreshingly, the older you get, the easier it's become to pull triggers. You concoct a plan. You sketch its details in your imagination. There's no need to rehearse, you have her in your sights.

Faith is straightforward, as women go. She has her own things, a profession, a home, a life that was as full as yours was before the two of you met. This wholeness attracted you. People are water, usually, and flow themselves into the empty spaces of others, their gaps and weakness and insecurity. You knew not to do this again. You corrected your search and this time you found a woman complete in her own right.

She comes from the suburbs that were the noose around your neighborhood's neck. Where you are originally of Suerte's flat lands, a kid from government housing, from the decrepit city center, she was the kind of black child who would remember vividly being the only one, and what white girls said about her hair, and how the white boys wanted to touch it, the covert racism of her classmates, their comments that never directly included her under the umbrella of their disdain yet condemned every helical strand in her DNA. She knows more than you ever will about Paris in 1990, the college customs of the Brits, the food ways of the French, the drunken holidays of the Germans. It is not that you cannot buy a ticket and go see all these things and more, but that she saw the world when she was young and everything was fresh and revelations were real.

She's younger, forty five to your sixty some years. Sometimes, caught at the right angle, in the right dress and bra, her breasts still float like the weightless orbs of twenty year old girls. She could pass for thirty, is still carded because of her cratered left cheek, the unwrinkled corners of her eyes and mouth, the unlined smoothness of her long neck, and the sharp lightness in her voice. Viewed from the retired side of retirement, she is still young enough to be compelled into the world by something more than quiet despair. That something more might be called hope. She is a little like Obama, you think sometimes, when you see him on TV, when you see her for lunch downtown in her suit amongst all the other ambitious thirty- and fortysomethings. But you like her more than Obama. Her rich, desert darkened skin, you can touch; her eyes you can judge to see what of you she understands, loves, hates; her words you can play over and again in your mind without the help of internet websites and political pundits analyzing the strategy of her rhetoric. She is different from you, but she is also here in this same suburb at this same moment— and when was the last time you related to anyone the way you do to her?

You are not a big fan of marriage, that's been your line for years now. The state should make no contracts dictating love; that's how you see it. But simply proposing love is like proposing to play Hamlet; it is words without deeds; it is action without any accountability. At its base, when you let yourself look past all the contracts and customs and governments and constitutions, what is marriage but a pact between two people held together only by themselves, not the state, not its papers, its laws, just two souls touching?

You were married before: 1975-1985. She is a white woman. Her name is Lindsey McConnell. When she was your wife, she went as Lindsey Deveraux, even took pleasure in calling herself Mrs. Vincent Deveraux in certain public settings. She was in the same class year as you at USC, came to the school at the same time as you and left on your arm. She has red hair and a dancer's legs and a laugh that flies away. You could have died then, enveloped in that laughter, those legs, her fully bloomed hips and breasts after the first pregnancy. Maybe you should have, just dropped out the game right then and there. She is a tenured university professor in New York now, but during your marriage to her she saw herself first as a wife and mother to your two children. She never stopped being the latter, but she did outgrow you, returning to SC with more than finding a man on her mind. Lindsey was nothing if not systematic in her ambitions, a husband, children, a Master's degree, a Ph.D., the proposal of a move back to her hometown in New York where her father was looking to hand over his business. Goddamn, you told her, white people just hand down your shit like money ain't a thing. I thought the Irish were broke! How'd all this inheritance come down in the first place? None of y'all know, nobody cares to ask. Bank heist, maybe? Probably had somethin' to do with 1750 and a plantation down in Dixie.

She was no fan of your racially charged quips. You were raising two mixed race daughters; this was no way to deliberate on the future or to respect your shared heritage. You were an asshole. No wonder thirty some years later Zanzibar and Paris, while they send presents and post cards and call every few weeks and make sure to see you when they come out to California, good daughters that they are, nevertheless have made their homes back East, Zanzibar in Providence, Paris in Syracuse. Both studied visual art and design in graduate school, would care which statue went where along a river walk, and seem, in their gentle way, to prefer their mother to you.

That relationship fractured and fell apart not because of skin and race, but because you were each outgrowing the other, becoming other to one another where before you were one and becoming other to the selves you had been before; you coming out of your conservatism, your John Wayne, your Stetsons, your European poetry; she out of her own unexamined life. She outstripped you in the classroom, left you to your Yeats—or was it Baraka by then? She became bi-coastal, raising the children in Orange County, raising Mr. McConnell's art gallery in the Catskills. You rooted yourself in San Suerte, believing that you could come to love this place more easily than you could come to know any other home: These dusty streets, these ramshackle shops, this town that hardly appears on maps, this frustration of a city was the stake you lashed yourself to.

The divorce was not finalized until June 15 1987. Paperwork and resentment are not accelerants. A year later, your mother passed away and you sensed yourself stumbling off-center, swaying incoherently under the influence of energies not your own. From this clumsy, self-battering sorrow, you realize now, you have never really recovered.

⁂

DESPITE YOUR DECISIVENESS, it still takes time to set a proper stage, the right ring, no diamonds, no African blood merchants, the right words, all four of them, five if you include her name, the right momentary lull in between headlong bursts of work that leave her drained and dazed and leave you detached, uninvolved, waiting patiently to regain her attention. You are not going to propose in public like some lame on a stadium Jumbotron at halftime of a Laker game. You invite her to your home, which is where your dates normally begin anyway. If you had come to her doorstep maybe she would have sensed something amiss and would have wandered around your request. Maybe she would have figured out that an old man without a purpose would see in her person that very meaning for himself. Maybe she would have been overjoyed or insulted; you're not sure. What you are sure of is that this is about more than a yes or a no, it is about those minutes you know that it will take her to wind through the quiet streets, five blocks in skirt and heels she will walk because she has never given in to the lethargy of the desert and the Southern California car culture. It is for the anticipation that will settle on your shoulders and in your throat that you have concealed this design. It is for the terrified panicked moment that you see her listing up your driveway in her stockinged feet, her purse and heels dangling desert flowers from her fingertips, her lips mouthing the remembered words to a song or a departmental review. Her mind might be in a million places; what you want is one more moment for yourself that is not slouching away from you even as it occurs: Turning and turning in the widening gyre, the falcon cannot hear the falconer.

You see her on the security camera that pans your long red clay driveway. At the porch steps, she leans down and places her heels on the ground and steps lightly into them, growing taller. She fusses with her hair and the long tips of her eyelashes as if the front door is a bathroom mirror. She stands there for what seems a very long time before she rings the doorbell. Your stomach revolves, reminding you of everything that you've consumed in the past few days. Everything inside you is alive; everything that has passed through you has left its taste, its fleshly signature. The falcon will hear you again.

You turn off the security cameras, all of them, and come down your stairs to the door. It has no window and for a second you imagine that the cameras may have lied, that her words on the phone earlier in the day may have lied, that she might not be here at all but rather the phantom ghost of your feelings now lying leaf-dead at your door. But the falcon has returned: She is perched there awaiting your movement, your word. You take a moment to look at her. The sun casts her something other than brown in its bracing light. You stand on the sheltered side of the open door, the sunlight deflected somewhat; but still, goddamn, the desert is hotter every summer, and your body is softer and weaker with the years, less resolute each time you encounter it. She does not seem to mind the sun. She is not asking to come inside. She just waits. And so you do as all men in this land do, take to one knee, the ring, held between two meaty fingers in your left hand. Your right extends to meet the long, bone-thin back of her hand. You trace its skeletal reaches and the veins that rise above the bones.

"Faith, will you marry me?"

Because of Faith: five words, not four, you think to yourself as you feel something catch in your chest. It is fast and sharp, but it is the accuracy of the attack, its seizure of you at your very center. You have felt pains in your chest before, points of abject weakness that dot your left breast. But these pains have always passed, inaccurate attempts against you. Now, though, you are being crushed by galactic hands. You are compressed into the space of your heart, where all life is predicated; you are compacted like months of landfill into this moment, everything at once, you and she and your love for her and your disavowal of everything less worthy than love, all of it now.

The hands that have crushed you lift what is left, your dismantled heart, your last moment alive, your claims upon love and greatness. You notice that you are pitching backward out of your crouch. Faith flails and cries and leaps upon you. She is screaming. She scrambles on to the great fallen branch of your body. She beats on your chest, her fists little but light knocking on something that is not a door. You are the falcon and she the falconer. She turns and turns about you, thinking to save you by paramedic, by CPR, by Samaritan miracle, the saviors that do not answer. You are good, you are already gone. The gyre was always infinite, you simply ceded to it now. You left without slouching. You did not belabor the moment, drawing things out in scattered stunted emotions. You were swift and final. You flew.

•

FUNERAL IN FRESNO

TOUISSANT'S GRANNY DIED AND went below ground in August 1991. At Fresno's Adventist Church, Touissant and his family and the whole Freeman clan came to lay their lady to rest; while meanwhile their old Rev. came to send her off in the timeliest manner possible. These weren't the most compatible ambitions, but the Rev. knew that there was such a thing as a badly executed funeral and he didn't want to preside over another such spectacle. Only a couple days before, he had overseen the funeral for a young lady who'd lived life too hard and too fast, segueing from a short childhood into an over-long adolescence, and finally a terrible death from the plague of plagues. Some things, the Rev. had learned, were best buried quick and not lingered over too long. But the funeral lagged and lagged, and dragged on well past tears and into numbness (though there were tears; one of the deceased's shady associates stumbled in her stilettos and managed to heave herself upon the coffin during recessional). And the whole thing eventually became analogous to the lady's sordid life and more sordid death. So now the Rev., who'd known Mae Truth for thirty years and more, was determined not to let a good woman's funeral go bad.

To that end, he ignored Mae's twin granddaughters, who were hissing audibly at each other in the front row, and ticked off his opening remarks with the rapid efficiency of an auctioneer. He'd always prided himself on his BCC status, black, Christian and charismatic, and arranged his sermons to accent those virtues. But now he reminded himself that such blessings were two-sided and that, matter-fact, he bore some of the blame for the excesses of the recent funeral. It was one of those sermons when the words ran away with him and he had become eloquent and lost his sense: *Their throat is an empty tomb*: Psalm 5:9. He should've heeded those sacred words, but the tragic nature of the deceased's life and death had stirred him to rambling.

Now, Mae Truth hadn't lived a life of sin so he wasn't moved to any eloquence, only a few appropriate words. She had been a good woman, he said, maybe a little sad here and there but that was to be expected amidst a bad world and bad men. None of the world's sin could bother her now that she was in heaven, he reasoned, so this was no time to be sad, let alone them excessive carryings on, he counseled the congregation; and that was all that needed to be said, he said.

He checked his timepiece: Now for the "Remembrances." L.A. Freeman sauntered forward with his usual smooth confidence. Even at his advanced age, so old and full of days, he remained exceptionally light on his feet, old Rev. noticed. Not even his wife's death, it seemed, could slow his roll or break his stride. An exacting union the two of them must have shared, one living a low-stress no-stress lark, the other bearing everything in her big breaking heart. Now L.A. was out a wife and he had no one to blame but himself. The best he could do for her now was give her a good sending-off, which was one thing L.A. almost surely would manage: he could still talk with the best, still retained his wit, rarely resorted to the obscurity of silence like so many men his age. If there was one thing Mae had always loved about her man it was that he was a wonderful talker. L.A., she used to say, had *his way* with words.

Now, the man with the words unfolded all six-foot-four inches of himself out of his seat, down the aisle and up to the pulpit. The Rev. stepped aside and passed off stage. Then he watched as L.A. reached one long thin hand into his pants pocket and came out with a badly wrinkled sheet of paper. The Rev. wondered just how long L.A. had been carrying it around with him, it was so crumpled up. He heard the granddaughters giggling and wanted to join them. Once L.A. began to speak it was clear that however worn the thing was, it hadn't been much time in the composing:

"Now," he intoned, coughing, clearing the years out his voice, "Now I done wrote this right here. I want y'all, all y'all to understand I wrote this here. Wadn't no one helpin me, no one overseein me like if I was a preacher had me a team sayin, go 'n put this here, put that there, makin it sound all pretty for me. Nah, I done this on my own, these is my honest to God words; if anyone here don' care for 'em it's they own misconceptions at work 'cause who here knew Mae Truth better 'n me? I challenge anyone here on *that*. I known the girl, what was it? When we get married? Long time, Jesus.

"I met her out the pen. Was goin to church, where all the fine unattached girls be. Spend all Sund'y mornin gettin dressed, show up on them church steps wit my handkerchief at twelve o'clock. Make like I been in there sweatin, worshippin wit the congregation. Mae had no idea I'd been in jumpsuits more 'n church pews, but, love. Lemme tell ya, she was the funniest chick in the world: couldn't take Birmingham, broke out wit the crop each year. Couldn't take Chicago, tested her religion. Why I'm so shocked by my boy Bobby jitterbug-ass. He was her favorite so I had always figured him for a prime square.

"But now, I finally brung her out here, came to this small Fresno world. Looked nice at a distance. But wouldn't you know it, found us a home, here, for when it was good times or bad, came through plenty 'a both. An' we made it unto death do us part. That's worth somethin', I hazard, no matter what nobody say," at which point his speech disintegrated into grumbling Alabaman obscurities and he seemed to grow tired and even serene.

Then his only son, Bobby, came forward. He was crying all down his cheeks even before he offered his words to the congregation. It wasn't easy to make out what he had to say, choked up as he was. But the Rev. listened close and came to understand that he had loved his mother deeply and suffered greatly with her passing: "What I, remember, is," he halted over each word, "is how much she loved us. How she would love us each and every day of her life. How, my Lord, she was my mother." He put his head in his hands to stifle down his tears, but his words still came out his throat with heat and hurt. "It was never easy, not in the places we lived. No rock to hide. Try and hide your face, rock yells up—"

Bobby paused. The mourners all exhaled. They needed that pause. Even the Rev. found himself gathering his wind and staring with rapt attention at the man falling apart before him; and the sense of embarrassment, like if he had happened in on a private moment, actually was greater than any feeling of pity or compassion. It was a sort of spontaneous disintegration, not only for Bobby, but for him, too, since his embarrassment and fascinated shame actually set back his punctual plan for a moment.

Bobby's shoulders shook and great old tears welled up in his eyes again. But his voice was steadier when he began to speak, and now there were a few murmured Amens urging him on. "I remember how she took to me, me being her only son. She treated me like a prince. My sisters, they'd get a little anxious, a little mad, but it was only love, I think"—Amen, someone shouted. "Rock yelled up, *no hiding place*; that's, that's how it goes"; he was losing his way again—"C'mon, son. C'mon, you almost home!"—"That's the song. Been, time..." His words trailed away into a no man's land of dry sobs. The Rev., who had never wept in public, wondered how much it must hurt the throat to cry dryly and speak all at the same time. He was full of fascination as he started toward the pulpit.

Bobby turned on him, his eyes red as brimstone. The Rev. hesitated again, shaken in the sight. It had been a long time since his own dungeon had shook and though he regularly witnessed the phenomenon in other people its intensity in Bobby Freeman touched him. Maybe because it was a man crying this time, maybe because it was Mae Truth's son, that harsh Lilly's husband. He wasn't sure what it was about Bobby's eyes that made him hesitate, but he drew back.

Then he remembered himself and kept on coming. He put a light hand on Bobby's shoulder and felt that shoulder fall. Old Rev. came closer to him, his hand still on his shoulder, until his considerable weight was up against Bobby and he could move him as he wished. He maneuvered him out the pulpit.

He waited a second to make sure the boy was alright; he watched him down the stairs and across the church till he folded his tall frame into the pew-space between his daughters. His wife was looking at him disapprovingly. The Rev. raised a hand to silence the whispers that filtered throughout the church—feeling like a judge now, returning the court to order—and looked out across the crowded building. As person after person noticed the widening silence and shut up their mouths and cast their eyes back on the Rev., old Rev. found himself casting his gaze out over them and wondering, What's left to say? There was, he remembered, still one more remembrance to be read. Then Lady would read the eulogy and the casket would be carried away, lowered into its grave. A song would be sung. Time was once again slipping through his fingertips, out of his control and expanding willy-nilly in all directions. He couldn't seem to orchestrate an efficient funeral no matter how hard he tried. His job, he decided, had grown progressively harder. *All things are full of labor*, he thought to himself, looking out at the individual faces, each one looking to him for some articulation of the whirlwind. Black, brown and white faces come to mourn and to question, with their eyes like searchlights upon him. *All things are full of labor*, he thought, and *Man cannot express it*: Ecclesiastes 1:8.

He felt a deep urge to read to them from Ecclesiastes so that they wouldn't be so damn ready to whisper this and that amongst themselves and then go look to him to confirm their agitated gossip about Bobby or Mae or God. The Rev. felt a sudden desire to shirk his responsibility, in so far as reassurance was that responsibility. He remembered how in certain translations Ecclesiastes began chapter 1, first verse, with the Preacher saying, "Nothing of nothings; Nothing of nothings, all is nothing." He hadn't read these translations and thus had no first-hand knowledge of them, but he had heard of them and now the thought of their unadulterated hopelessness consoled him. He wasn't in a good state to be leading anybody, despite his title. He had no special words, certainly no assurances other than that a funeral was no place to linger, because time was short, time and life were short and even death came and passed as quickly as a moment.

He had heard scientific theories positing that time was not linear but in fact proceeded parallel to itself in never-ending repetitions so that as soon as people died, they returned to life's beginnings and re-lived their time on earth. By this logic, no one ever really died, they only passed between similar universes in a sort of infinite renewal. The Rev. didn't know what to make of such thinking, he didn't know whether to be attracted or repelled by the idea that Mae Truth had returned to the womb as she breathed her last and he mourned her death. The mourners needed him now. Their big, tearful eyes said so. But he had nothing for them. He called on the Freeman boy, who was scheduled to read the last remembrance: "Touissant." He looked after him. "Touissant, son."

It was absurd to call on a child at such a crucial moment, with so many needful eyes turned his way. It felt deeply absurd and deeply wrong, but also somehow appropriate that it should go like this, not because the child would have anything meaningful to say to the congregation, no, but because he himself was tired and old and sad and too jaded for tears. He looked out at the questioning faces one more time as he summoned the child.

He hardly knew this Touissant boy. Mae loved him, he knew that. But Mae loved everybody and the boy was her only son's only son, so there was no way she wouldn't love him. She probably would've loved him if he were the devil incarnate, considering. Hopefully, he was a good child, but the Rev. had his suspicions to the contrary: children were forever hindering things, crying through sermons, leaping into caskets, disrespecting constraint and disregarding time. Moreover, this boy was probably a particular trouble: Bobby and Lilly left Fresno to get married and raise their kids in one of those Southern California suburb-cities, the Rev. couldn't recall its name, though he was generally suspicious of all suburbs, cities and things beyond the grapevine. Bobby and Lilly were born-Fresnoans but they'd slipped that yoke and the way they acted now, you would've figured them for a couple born and reared in Hollywood or somewhere else fancy. But now Bobby seemed to dissemble from the word go, and Lilly, well she was wearing an orange scarf over her black clothes; the article curled around her perfect neck, accenting her fine lines and showing up the imperfection in all the other women. Like she needed to remind everyone she'd switched cities.

And now watching their child pass up the aisle and onto the stage, into the pulpit, fascinating every eye with his approach, it was like the Rev. could see the whole grapevine being burnt under in flames. The boy was only about as tall as a stalk of cotton in the field, but the way he held his head so high, his back so straight, could make you forget how small and young he was. And then up at the pulpit the way his brown eyes trained on the distance before him it seemed as if he were seeing through and into something deeper further on, beyond the Rev and the congregation and the church and funeral altogether. He watched as Touissant found the footstool hid inside the pulpit hollow. The child hopped on to the support and adjusted the microphone without help. Then he started to undo the origami folds of a paper he'd taken from his pocket. He raised it up in the air, in the light, then set it down, roaming his intense eyes across it as if inspecting it for impurity. He took his time, lingering coolly over his preparations. Like he knew what he was doing.

"She was perfect when she was with me," the boy began. "She was perfect. She would run her fingers into my hair and we would sit up late listening to the radio or the record player or the wind. She'd tell me how special me and my sisters were to her. I'll always remember that. When me and my sisters are all older and far away from here and in a whole different world, we'll remember. Like statue time, remember. So I'm not sad, I'm not crying or whatever. I'm happy."

Old Rev. felt as old as the hills right then. Here was this child saying everything he had lost the precision and the passion to say himself. The boy was an angel of a future that might not contain the old Rev. and, knowing, or at least feeling this, he sensed time itself descend upon him in one fell fall. He wasn't sure how long the youngin' would speak, but he didn't seem at a loss for words.

The Rev. left his seat on stage and walked behind the curtain into the dark backstage area. He had to be careful not to wander blindly into sharp objects or things fragile enough to easily dislodge or topple to the ground with embarrassing crescendo. It reminded him of being a young father, having to get up in the middle of the night in the pitch black to do this or that for his son, and praying he did not step on another Lego or Lincoln log. He still didn't know if those things transmitted toxins, tetanus, some devilment or another that Ralph Nader might've warned the world about when the Rev. was too busy serving God to notice. It was not uncommon for the Rev. to do this, his parishioners were familiar with him taking a moment to himself during proceedings. He took a deep, solid breath into his lungs, just as his meditation teacher had taught him to do. The Buddhists were all unrepentant heathens but damned if they didn't know how to relax well, the Rev. could not but concede that truth.

He would still be able to hear the child speak from the alleyway out back so he opened the exit door and walked outside. It was a hot wind-swept afternoon. Stepping out from the church felt like walking right into the blistering path of a blow dryer set to high. He gritted his teeth and squinted his eyes.

"Hey now," a sluggish, desiccated voice called in his direction.

"Hell if it ain't him," another said. "Hey Rev. We L.A.'s friends."

Figures, thought the Rev. G—damn figures.

"Ain't the service still under way?" a third voice asked. "What you doin outside?"

The Rev. stopped and opened his eyes enough to see three men he recognized but vaguely. They appeared above the heat waves and the film of windblown dust ghostlike as apparitions. They were not churchgoing men, he knew that much. The smells of liquor and marijuana wafted toward him. Sometimes the back alley was redolent of piss and other times of sewage so, judged against that, the hooch and reefer weren't so bad. But there was propriety and respect to think about, too. The Rev. was having a bad day and the sun-drenched sight of so many old men carousing like teenage boys out back of his church did not help. It only made him feel all the older and feebler for not joining in or mustering the strength to stop it. "Don't you think it's a tad early for smoking and drinking, brothers? Sun's out." he finally said from a distant, defiant but not wholly responsive part of himself.

"We ain't tryina profane no church service," the first man, who was dressed in an old gray frayed Goodwill-looking three-piece allowed. "That's why we came out back."

The logic escaped old Rev., or logic escaped the old men; one way or the other, it wasn't working.

"I appreciate the effort, but why do it at all? Especially the smoking?"

"Some us prefer the ci-gar, some prefer the reefer," the man replied.

"It just doesn't really seem to honor the deceased, you catch my drift?"

The three men, each of them suited, each of them hatted, each of them shoe-polished and cuff-linked and bow-tied, each of them siphoned to the dry, withered edge of their money for these old airs and this drink and this smoke, squinted back. "Look," said one, "if Mae was alive, if she was here, she'd be out here, not in there."

The Rev. was about to retort, from rote reprimand, but those words caught him unexpected—he had been about to say that Mae Truth was a woman after his own heart, after the church's own heart, and Jesus and Joseph and the whole nine yards, but then the man had said the last thing he had expected him to say. That Mae Truth would be out back of the church where the liquor was downed and the smoke floated about was news to him. It flew against all he knew of the woman, every experience he had ever had of her. These were L.A.'s friends, he realized—he recognized their faces now, faces of factory and field men whom he had not seen in a decade and more, but who were as well-acquainted him to them and them to him as every childhood and adolescent memory. These were old Fresno men, brothers he had known since grade school. They had not gone anywhere, including church. They were just as they had always been, men who labored the day away hard and strong and unrecalcitrant on the floor, on the line, in the patch, behind the plow; who knew good and well not to waste the night, which was precisely when old Rev. typically tucked himself away at home, save for the holy roller revivals he now and then still got dragged out to perform.

He had been one of these men when he was young and still

unskilled in the scripture. He had worked the floor, worked the line, chopped heads from chickens and loaded watermelon and cut glass. But the Rev. had moved on, gone to seminary, got posted-up with a church and all in his era own hometown, and had moved out of the West Side and into the Sanger suburbs. No wonder he hadn't recognized these brothers on first blush.

"It ain't that Mae was a smoker or a drinker," brother Lewis in the gray suit said. "She weren't. It's jus she wadn't the sort to separate herself. Mae liked her a field nigger, didn't mind her a street nigger, jus as much as she kept time wit y'all churchin negroes. That's why she loved L.A. wild ass so much."

Just then, right when old Rev. was about to concede, say "Fair enough, fair enough," he heard his cue—the child had finally stopped preaching. He didn't have time to tell the men to keep on with their bad selves, or that he remembered them one and all, or that every alleyway served some purpose in God's creation. He had to get back to work. The silence called.

HOMECOMING

I REMEMBER THINKING IT was an all right house, but I wouldn't want to die in a hole-in-the-ground like Raisin City, that's what I remember. I remember thinking Laz and PoDog must be crazy, they seemed so determined to die there, that's what I remember.

Uncle Laz's home was a low-ceilinged, narrow-built, well-kept place. It lay up a long dirt road and dirt driveway, and when we got there besides the house the only thing anywhere was a sportscar sitting out front. She was dressed in shiny blue clothes that made her look like she'd been illustrated into the world, a shining dark lady. Her sunglasses and baseball cap didn't let me see her face

"Jayson." Dad tapped me on the shoulder. "That girl sitting on her car, that's your oldest cousin, your cousin Nisa. You two knew each other about ten years ago. You were two or so and she was barely a teenager herself back then," he said.

"But she had cold down to an art, even then," mom said.

"She wasn't so bad. I was talking to Fred yesterday. He told me she graduated early, full-time editor job. Too smart for this family." Dad laughed.

Nisa waved our car to a stop and when dad parked the car, he was the first one out, striding over to her, reaching up and hugging her. He smiled and laughed. She turned her cap backward and kissed him on the cheek. Mom got out last. She stood halfway between the two cars and told Nisa if she wanted a hug from her, she'd have to climb down from the car and meet her halfway.

"He's dying in there," Nisa responded. She motioned over her shoulder at the house. "Not in the house itself," she explained, "but in the shed behind it. He had uncle Laz put a bed back there for him and he's been lying out there for three days now."

"Why's PoDog want to be in that rickety old shed for?" Mom frowned. "The shed is older than the house."

"He had Laz put him out there," Nisa shrugged. " 'Cain't let you see me with one leg. Gonna die on my own damn terms.' "

Mom didn't know how to respond to that and didn't. After a minute, Nisa broke the stillness, hopping down from the car, walking past my parents toward me. "I remember you, my best cousin," she smiled. She bent down and hugged me. "Hug me back, honey, c'mon now. You want to go play basketball right now, you and me? I'm dressed for it."

I couldn't see PoDog's shed from where I stood. I didn't answer Nisa.

"It's 8:15 a.m! Why do you want to play basketball at 8:15 a.m?" mom cried. Then she waved her hands up at the sky or something, to prove that it was too early for basketball games.

"I've been in Raisin City hanging out with Laz and PoDog since yesterday," Nisa said. "I'm ready to be young and active." She paused, then added, "I got here a day early and I've been suffering the consequences. My parents asked me to hurry and get here before PoDog died and they haven't even come yet." She quieted, momentarily. Gently, she lay her hand on my head. "Anyway, I found the only basketball court in town. Me and the little man can use it."

"8:15," mom said again. "Doesn't that seem early to you, Nisa, or are you just running on a different clock than the rest of us?"

But Nisa'd already begun to drift off. She drifted over to the fence, unlatched it and disappeared into Laz's backyard. Past the open fence door I could see part of PoDog's shed, its metal a gentle, pale blue in the early sunlight. Nisa came back, closing the fence door behind her—the shed went away—she was cradling a deflated-looking basketball, holding it close to her chest and fixing her eyes on it like it might die if she dribbled it or let it out of her sight. "I know it's early," she said, "but it's play, it's for the sake of play." Then she suddenly tossed the basketball straight at me. It hit my hands, stinging me as I instinctively gathered it into my chest; I took my eyes off the fence and the shed behind the fence and followed her to her car.

"You look at the houses out here and you think, what's gonna happen when the wind blows?" Nisa pushed her sunglasses up onto her forehead and arched her eyebrows. Her eyes were tired and red. "You'd think PoDog would have a better plan to get out of Raisin City than running circles around a track, right?"

I remember not wanting to disappoint her with my answer; I didn't answer.

"It's O.K., it's not imperative you have an opinion. But tell me, has your mother ever told you the secret about men?"

"No," I answered, my eyes making a diagonal dash for the car floor so as to hide my confusion from my cousin.

"Poor child!"

"Me?"

"I better fill you in on the truth before your dad and your uncles put all that archaic stuff in your head."

I had one dad and four uncles: Uncle Ronny, who was half my uncle and half somebody else's something, Frederick, who was Nisa's father, Laz, who would die in Raisin City, and PoDog, who was maybe dying in Raisin City right now. "The truth?" I wondered aloud.

"Yeah, about guys: they cause most of the problems in this world. Trust me; trust me even if I seem strange. Can I help seeming strange when I'm right and everybody else is wrong?" She slowed the car and rolled through a stop sign. She pointed down the road at a high metal gate surrounded by dead, gray weeds. "There's the court. But about guys," she steered the wheel with her knees and played with her sunglasses until they fell back over her eyes, "Your uncles are gonna tell you all about Mother Earth, Sister Death, how death and girls are one and the same. But look at PoDog, he brought this on himself—and I bet you he turns around and blames it on some girlfriend from 1975."

"Is uncle PoDog gonna die?"

I think she started to say yes, but then the car came to a stop right before the dead reach of the weeds. She opened her door and stepped out into the weeds and ran her hands down her gray legs. "Man, my legs are as ashy as yours," she said, whistling the words out.

I got the basketball from the backseat and we waded over to the open gate. By the time we got to the gate our legs were even ashier. "How can we pretend to be Allen Iverson and Sheryl Swoopes with ashy legs?" Nisa mused. "Do you think Iverson would come out on national television with ashy legs?"

The courts were slippery with sand and dangerous to walk on, let alone play basketball. So we used our feet as brooms and swept the sand into far-off piles as best we could. "Sheryl looks so regal. She's classically contoured. It wouldn't do to play her and be slipping," Nisa said. "On the other hand, Iverson's whole game is on the edge between balance and a fall."

Nisa showed me how to dance along Iverson's edge. "You rhythm dribble and you shake your hips like a girl in a music video. Watch." She demonstrated.

Iverson would go easy on girls, Nisa explained. Then she beat me five games in a row. "See," she said, cradling the basketball so tenderly again, "it's not the YMCA, it's not about who wins and who loses."

That made no sense to me, it only made me angry: I wanted to throw something. But she was holding the basketball. I tried to bite my lip off while I stared at her, which I think scared her a little because she started to dribble the ball again and we played one more game, for Iverson's ego.

When we got back to Laz's it was past twelve o'clock. Several cars were rowed in his dirt driveway where before there had only been Nisa's little blue sportscar. "Shit," she said, breaking the silence: the whole family had arrived and now she would have to park out on the street.

"Make sure you lock your door, sweetie," she said over her shoulder. Then she was out of the car and onto the crowded driveway. She slowed down and let me catch up to her. "You're twelve. I'm guessing you probably wouldn't want to sleep in a bedroom with your parents? Want mine?"

"Don't you want your bedroom?"

"I'm not going to be staying for the funeral," she said, "I don't think I'll need the bedroom tonight." She got quiet for a second, something she did whenever the conversation turned toward uncle PoDog and death. "Being here, I feel like I see my features in every face, except PoDog's. But it's him I have everything in common with. The way people love him and don't know how to show it, I feel that." She cut across the driveway to the cars parked in blocks of two. "Look, this is my parents' car." She ran her finger across the thin coat of gray dirt that sheathed the black Lexus. The car stood out amongst all the old flatbed trucks in the driveway. She put her finger on one truck painted in chestnut and rust colors, its bed walled by a wooden fence: "That's Ronny's. He calls it his skillet. He's from Alabama. You know," she added, sighing like a whistle, "I doubt PoDog ever bought a car."

"Why won't he buy one?" I asked.

"Lots of reasons, probably. You have to have money to have a car and he never had much of that. But more than that, you've got to care for a car like it's something precious or you're not a good American. PoDog cared about his legs like that and now that he doesn't have his legs to care about I think it's like he lost his citizenship." She looked at me. "Maybe it was too hard to care like that again. C'mon, let's go meet our people."

When we went inside, Nisa wanted to show me my bedroom, but her mother wanted her to make lunch for everyone. She needed Nisa to thaw the chicken and skim the fat off it.

Besides frozen chicken, the only thing in Laz's refrigerator was a bowl of uncooked sweet potatoes. "I'll handle the sweet potatoes," Nisa's mother said. It was uncle Laz's house and his food but he refused to cook, not for himself, not even for PoDog. Laz was fasting—he didn't call it fasting, but he wanted to lose weight and had decided not to eat for three days. Apparently, the night before, too tired to cook for herself and PoDog, Nisa had had to drive into Fresno for fast food.

After she thawed the chicken and skimmed away its fat, Nisa stuck the chicken in the stove and walked down the hall. I followed her down the narrow way to the final door on the left, where she had slept the night before. Past the final door, there was a screen that opened on to the backyard. As we walked down the hall, we could see PoDog's shed gleaming in the sunlight.

Nisa opened the door into the bedroom. Her purse and two suitcases were scattered across the wood floor. "You feel like you can sleep in here, cousin?"

"It's fine."

"You can sit down," she said, motioning toward a suitcase. "I couldn't sleep in here last night, won't try tonight," she said, as she melted down to the floor under the spell of her fatigue. "Maybe if we imagine we're in a real nice place it'll seem cooler, nicer. You gonna help me imagine?"

I lay flat on the ground like a snow angel without wings and tried to imagine the world the way my cousin could. She could dream up all kinds of places that were nicer and cooler and more beautiful and more solacing than where we were and she could describe them for me down to their closest, comforting detail. But I wasn't as good at the game. It wasn't that I lacked an imagination: I kept imagining the shed in the backyard vanishing in a cloud of Raisin City dust. There would be thunder then the shed would vanish. That was how we would know that PoDog had died. But aside from that, nothing came to my mind except thoughts of home, far away.

I was still trying to imagine or understand why anyone would want to die in Raisin City, in a metal shed, when mom walked past our open door and looked in. She held a tin pan in her hands, a whole sweet potato pie with a crust kneaded into little hoop earrings overflowing the plate's edges. Mom peered at us through the open door: "Nisa, you just stuck the chicken in the stove. You never even turned the stove on," she said. She was staring at Nisa: her eyes were deep with something. But Nisa wouldn't stare back at her. Her eyes were closed like she was asleep, like she was off somewhere else, imagining. After a silent minute, mom went on down the hall, out to the backyard. "PoDog's gonna throw something at her." Nisa chimed, her eyes still closed. "He threw an empty flower pot at me last night when I tried to bring him that fast-food."

"Why doesn't he want to eat?"

"Oh, it's not that he doesn't want to eat. I'm sure he's hungry! It's just his ego. He refuses to let any woman see him. 'Cain't let you see me,' he said to me.

Let's just hope he misses your mother like he missed me with the flower pot." Then she got up and closed the bedroom window and drew the blinds.

"*Nisa,* that'll make it hotter!"

"*Shhhh.* What's the difference between one-hundred ten and one-hundred fifteen degrees? This way, there will be less noise, more silence to think."

A few seconds after Nisa said that, mom rushed back through the screen door, up the hall. I looked up and saw her pass our open door: cinnamon-colored hoop earring crust was stuck to her dress; she waved her hands in the air frantically.

I rushed out of the bedroom, up the hall to where the rest of the family was. Mom was in a corner, crying. Dad and uncle Laz were holding her, explaining how PoDog didn't want any woman to see him now, not even his sister. "Anyways," Laz shrugged, "PoDog's dyin from the inside out. What's he gonna do with a whole pie?" I was relieved. For a moment, I had thought she was crying because uncle PoDog had already died.

"Not yet," Nisa said. She was waiting for me in the bedroom doorway. "Not sure why she's so upset. He's probably got a little dementia, reverting to babyhood, throwing crap." She pointed into the backyard where two paint cans and a yardstick lay in the weeds between the shed and the house. Nisa walked back into the bedroom, and I followed: "Nisa?"

"Yes?"

I didn't ask the question that I wanted to but she figured out what was in my head.

"I don't understand her and she doesn't understand why I don't understand her. Even when I was little, I would go to hug her and we'd hug far away stretching our arms out, like this, straining. I think it's because she's really from here and I don't even know how the houses stay standing and how the people don't starve and how the summer doesn't burn everything to ashes in this terrible little place."

I was completely lost in her words so I just nodded at her.

"You dig?" She smiled warmly. "You don't dig. It's O.K., I don't either. How come they don't all just check out like PoDog, as hard as this place is? I don't get it. But this place doesn't get me either. We can't survive each other very long."

The word "survive" made me think even more closely about my dying uncle.

"Why do they call him PoDog?" I suddenly wanted to know. "Is that his real name?"

Nisa went and lay down on the bed, on her stomach. "Hope not. That would be unfortunate." She paused, moved her sunglasses onto her forehead. "I wouldn't know why they call him PoDog. That's the kind of thing our Raisin City relatives know. Like I said, I don't get any of it." She looked over her shoulder at me. "Do I look Raisin City to you?"

She wore a royal blue Lakers jersey and royal blue shorts that hung down to her shins. She had tucked her shoulder-length hair under a sky-colored scarf. She didn't look one bit Raisin City. But I knew that she knew what the name meant. I waited on her answer.

She said something about how a woman can walk over a line and she's just a mystery after that. She flipped over onto her back: "Boys never become mysteries, I guess. They just change names or something. Even Podog is just another word for prairie dog. I'm guessing you've never seen a prairie dog? You're not from here, why would you? You're not missing anything. Prairie dogs are fast. Our uncle was once very fast, fast like a prairie dog." Then she turned back onto her stomach and took a piece of triangle-folded paper out of her wallet. She unfolded it and for a while she just jotted on the paper and was silent. "You hungry?" she asked later. I shrugged. She got up from the bed, left the bedroom and went up the hall. She came back with a plate of food.

She let me sit on her bed and eat, and she gave me the piece of paper, which folded back in on itself at the creases like a flower closing itself up. "Here, since you're so hard after facts, honey. I'm headed outside, I need fresh air."

I heard her flat-soled shoes scrape against the wooden floor and then I heard the screen door open and shut. I didn't think she was going out there to try to see uncle PoDog. Later, I would learn that that wasn't it because after dad went out back, he told us how Nisa was just sitting in the backyard in a lawn chair. "Just sleepy, I guess" he shrugged.

"Just strange is my guess," mom said.

"Well, PoDog's asleep too," dad said. "But before he went, he said, 'Tell 'em I want the men out here; read me somethin' scriptural if my strinth be up.'"

I knew scriptural meant the Bible. He wanted us to read the Bible to him. For now, I read the closing-flower piece of paper:\

Facts:

PoDog was triple state champion as a junior in high school. He beat Warren Edmonson 4 times that year.

His hamstring blew out when he was a senior.

He went to junior college. He tore his other hamstring trying to run down Tommie Smith. Then he quit running because he needed money and the last way to make money back then was to run track.

He grew up with Olympic champions, outran some of them. But he never made it to the Olympics, or even out of Raisin City. He stayed here because here people knew what the name PoDog meant.

He drank and went homeless and managed to get gangrene in the hottest town in California and had to have his leg amputated. When the doctors told him he needed an amputation, he refused.

Uncle PoDog woke up around three in the afternoon and hollered from the shed until Nisa woke and went in the house to gather the men, including me. We went to the shed where PoDog, a withered man with banana-colored eyes, lay dying beneath several layers of bed covers. I remember thinking, God, he must be so hot under those covers in this small old shed.

Uncle Laz didn't own a Bible. Nobody had brought one with them either. PoDog started to mutter things under his breath, under his bedsheets: they weren't words, just sad sounds. While he went on muttering and the rest of us tried to recall specific prayers, I guess Nisa was out on the lawn chair listening to what was going on. She entered the shed abruptly and made her way straight to uncle PoDog's bedside. She was holding one of those little green Bibles that they sell on freeway off-ramps and at airports. She held the Bible in her cupped hands like food on a pretty tray. "Here," she said, and for the first time her voice sounded slightly nervous. "I bought it before I got on the plane. I read some of it during my flight. You know, It gets really repetitive, this man was born, then that one, then the next. And the stories seem like they all end the same. But it's poetic."

PoDog wouldn't take the Bible from her. He closed his eyes and sank further beneath the bed and bed covers. Her dad went over to Nisa and whispered something in her ear. He put his hands on her shoulders and led her away from the bed. She stopped sliding her feet when they reached the doorway. She stopped and took off her scarf, and her thickly tangling, dreadlocking hair fell down to her shoulders. "It's all a mess," she said, gesturing at her splash of matted, wild locks. He walked her outside.

"Least he ain't throw nothin at her," Ronny from Alabama said.

"Wouldn't matter." Uncle Laz shook his head. "PoDog throw like a chick."

He was sitting right there but it was like he wasn't the way they were talking about him.

Uncle Frederick returned with the little green Bible and gave it to PoDog, who sat up on his elbows and read from I forget which apostle until he was either too tired or too hoarse to keep going. "Y'all ain't my apostles," he mumbled, "Y'all can leave, as you feel." Then he fell asleep, an act much easier to understand. We did what we knew how to do: we filed past his bed one by one and kissed him good afternoon and goodbye.

Dad walked with me back through the yard into the house. He put his hands on my shoulders when he began to cry.

"I like Nisa," I said haltingly.

"So do I," dad said.

We past by her open bedroom door. She lay on the bed on her stomach. She'd put her scarf and hat back on. She turned her eyes up at us as we passed.

At dinner that night, uncle Laz finally ended his fast. He announced that he was ready to cook, which would have been nice of him had he announced it before Nisa and her mom had fried the chicken. That fact didn't seem to disturb him, though. "Sixty-four hours!" he shouted. "Golden hours!" He looked around smiling at everybody seated at the dinner table. "Lost five pounds, and it shows."

"I hope you hallucinate, fall out next time you try that stunt," mom said. "Teach you to kill that foolishness. Sixty-four hours, Lord."

"Bullshit fasting," Ronny added.

"Forcin' other people to cook for you in a house you own." Aunt Rita sighed. "Boy, you should be ashamed."

"Not as shamed as I am of my half-brother Ronny here. He's up in my house cursing before mixed company," uncle Laz said.

"What's mixed company, dad?" I asked.

"Men, women and children," dad whispered in my ear.

"Cursing before women and children," Laz harangued.

"Women, children, same category, right?" Nisa fixed uncle Laz with a cold stare.

"You are beyond frigid," mom snapped at her.

"Why's it always gotta be the girl who gets blamed for everything?"

"I can't even understand half what she says," mom said to everyone other than Nisa.

"Laz boy, I never," Aunt Rita began, then stopped short. "Don't look at me funny like that neither."

"I can't understand why PoDog won't let me see him," mom cried. "It's, it's not right."

"Girl, get over your damn self," aunt Lena said.

"A man's final wishes is to be honored," Ronny said.

"More cursing?" uncle Laz lamented.

"I'm going to go take PoDog some food," mom said. Uncle Frederick put his hand on mom's shoulder: "How about you let me do that." He left the table, put a piece of chicken on a plate and walked down the hall.

"Your uncle PoDog used to *shine*," dad said, looking at me.

"He was beautiful," Aunt Rita seconded.

"Almost body-snatched Tommie Smith at the West Coast Relays," Ronny said.

"Simply beautiful." Mom sighed. "It was different times, girl. Grape picking, cotton picking down this damn valley, sweating the Messicans; all of us poor and losing, and this one boy shining. You can't understand."

Nisa didn't answer back.

And the table lapsed into an extended silence.

Then Uncle Frederick returned. He slapped Laz upside his head. "PoDog's still holding on," he informed the table. "He's still holding steady."

"He needs someone to stay with him, to hold his hand," mom said. Ronny got up from the table and went down the hall.

Uncle PoDog's brothers spent the night on rotation in and out the shed. I stayed in the house and played card games with Nisa. I was Bill Gates, she said, and she was the Anti-Trust lawsuit. "Severe justice," she said.

I lost hand after hand and started getting real tired. Nisa was talking at Laz, playing the college-educated dozens on him to keep them both awake.

By ten o'clock I couldn't do a ripple shuffle without dropping a card on the floor face up. "You don't have to stay up for me." She yawned. "You have a room of your own now." She bent over and picked the joker from between two loose floorboards.

"Isn't that your room, though?" Laz wondered.

She waved the question off then waved me goodnight. She looked at

Laz. "C'mon, old man. So old, when you got your first paycheck you went and bought your freedom."

Laz laughed a real, unleashed laugh.

"I know you're not that old, brother. I'm just saying, Raisin City scares me. I thought I saw the Klan on the way in. They were looking at me hard, but when I started talking they figured I was a white girl and let me through."

Nisa turned and sat backwards in the chair, facing Laz, and dealt the cards.

In the night, I spread my clothes on the cold floorboards and lay down naked and aching in the darkness. I seemed to stand at an edge, a cusp, an inch outside ecstasy. I jacked off until I spent myself across the floorboards and lunged ecstatically downward into sleep.

The sound of Nisa's bare feet woke me, and bore me up out of hellfire. I could hear her, sense her somewhere near me, on the other side of my window. It was night still. She slid her bare feet through the dead weeds, making them crackle with her slow disturbance. I sat up from my mattress of clothes and stared at the window. In the spaces between the drawn blinds I could see her: she wore the jersey like a dress, down to her thighs, but other than that she was naked, I think. She'd let her hair loose to sit on her shoulders. I watched her slide through the yard, to PoDog's shed. When she was about thirty yards away from the shed, I threw on my day's shirt and slacks and snuck barefoot out of the bedroom, down the long dark hallway and out into the backyard. By the time I got there, I could see her in the moonlight: she shimmered along the shining length of the shed and the further away she went, the darker it got, and the more naked her shimmering image appeared. I tiptoed out into the yard and hid inside a low lemon tree. The skinny branches and little leaves embraced me like arms and hands and I was on earth and I was warm again.

I watched her go into the shed doorway and knock on the open door until it swung with the impact of her small fist. The sound of the knock bounded cartoonishly along the metal walls until it resonated throughout the yard and the night. PoDog sat up and stared at her. Uncle Frederick, whose meaty brown hand extended across the space of doorway never moved, never woke, as if Nisa's knock was not for him. Then PoDog collapsed back into the bed, and his heart must have stopped.

I waited. I was surprised how tired I was. After a silent while, I could hear Nisa's feet sliding through the yard, away from the shed. I peered between lemon leaves and saw her again. There were tears as clear and fine and bright as crystals in her eyes. In her arms, she carried PoDog's bed covers. There were so many bed covers that they overflowed her arms; they draped her naked body and trailed along the dirt like the train of a wedding gown. She sat down in the lawn chair, the covers gathered to her chest and wreathed round her waist and I could see how her legs had fallen out cold and exposed and how they were running in place. She sat in the lawn chair, her head in her hands and her hair flowing before her face in moon-white snake coils. I was warm within the lemon tree branches. I could feel earth tremors beneath me, trembling ground. The earth was black and warm, but I didn't want to stay out there all night. I waited till I could see Nisa's shoulders droop; then I knew for certain that she was asleep and I could sneak back inside.

But I couldn't sleep alone. Every time I closed my eyes PoDog sat up in front of me, and then promptly exploded into a billion bright nothings. I lay down to sleep on the floor in my parents' bedroom and when they saw me they understood that PoDog had gone.

The visit started to remind me of things, like the day when my teacher decided to teach us about slavery. We had been learning about bats and bugs and then one day we came in and sat down and she made us watch this video where whites sailed to Africa and made the blacks into slaves, whipped them, chained them by their necks and put them on boats, raped the black girls and all kinds of other stuff. Me and the white kids all sat there, learning to hate our ancestors, hate history, hate the whole world and the way things were, just like now everything about Raisin City had turned terrible but I couldn't just get up and go home and forget it all.

In the morning, mom yelled at Nisa because she was leaving before the funeral. When asked why she didn't want to stay, Nisa just shrugged: "You know how kids say *because.* Because, I mean, he's gone now, right?"

Mom sprang at her, knocked off her sunglasses and scratched her face.

Nisa fended her away, knelt and picked up the glasses. She was rubbing the lenses with one hand, her face with the other. But she wasn't fazed. There was something about Nisa that wasn't with the family, that had left long ago, and was lost to their knowing. But I loved her. "I was in love with him, too," she whispered to mom; then she fitted the glasses back in place and went home.

BY THE LEMON TREE

THE SUN HEAVES ITS harvest upon the great valley, the infinite farm land of Fresno and the lands beyond Fresno, the San Joaquin, the brown heartland of America. Verdant as any grape field worked over by migrant hands sun up to sun down, is a cemetery space, its very existence one of a slim few necessary concessions the growers have made to a god beyond green dollars. This consecrated space is all slow valleys and gentle rises and rich, deep earth. There are flowers here, and high, weather-worked trees shaped like perfect vases, or powerful, curving amazons.

Frank Hardeman didn't live at or near that cemetery. He lived on the westside of Fresno, where there was more cement than serenity. He lived in an enduring old home, low-lying, more filled with memories than amenities. He lived with the way things were. He knew about the beautiful burial ground on the outskirts of Fresno. He had known many people who were buried there now. But he had never set foot on those peaceful hills, not even for close friends.

"That's a one-way street, far as I'm concerned," he told his brother. "You go in, might as well be coffin carried."

"What if I were to die?" Wesley, Sr. wondered.

"Whose problem does that sound like?"

"Man, you're always having to be so cold."

That had been their conversation over the phone in April when an eighty-three-year-old woman on Frank's street had died and Frank incurred the wrath of anybody in the neighborhood who cared enough when he categorically refused to watch her get shelved away, as he put it. A few months later, deep in summer, Wesley, Sr. was telling his two grandchildren what he had told the culprit himself: that his brother had a personality like sharp ice and dry brush. "I think the way people kick up dust out there is affecting that old man," he said. "He's been bad of late."

"Maybe he should move away. Then he'll feel better," ten-year old Wesley said from the driver's side seat of the car. They were heading to Frank's place, a summer vacation of sorts.

"Nah, I think it's a permanent state of funk. Anyway, he's too vain about his house and his tenure there and his damn garden to move." Wesley, Sr. laughed.

"Uncle Frank's house ain't that great," Thalia said.

"Don't let him hear you say that, least don't let him hear you say it ain't as nice as ours. He'll make you weed that backyard till midnight."

From the backseat, Thalia started up, her voice thin and not loud, but happier than her grandfather's and three years more confident than her brother. "I do like his house," she corrected herself. "I remember it from the last time we was there. The hallway after his front door, it was narrow kind of, an' the rooms that opened out the hallway, they was like cardboard cut-outs: they was small but they was neat too. The two walls that make the long hallway got all kinds 'a African, Asian things standin' on mantles. They got pictures of our family, old pictures of some busted-lookin' old people, prob'ly from back before the Civil War if they had cameras back then. They some old relatives: I got no idea who they are. An' there's one 'a me with my brother from last year, last time we came to visit. Then there's all the pictures that's just Uncle Frank posted-up, flossed-out in his church clothes, even though I bet none 'a them pictures was even took on a Sunday.

"But the hallway ain't what I like. I just be rememberin' them pictures. Then, after the hallway, it's like two rooms. On the right's the kitchen, small, nice like everythin' else. It's got that oak sign hangin' over the stove, says, GOD BLESS OUR HOME, or somethin' else religious like that from back when Aunt C. was still alive. Then they got they names done under the sign an' some paintings too. There's them store-bought paintings, some jazz-type goins on, one's called Georgia in the Summer. The living room right next to it, to the kinda left, it got that ugly green rug I told him wadn't no good 'cause it's green an' ugly. Then there's the fireplace an' the old couch an' the creaky backdoor that goes out to the backyard."

"You remember everythin," Wesley said to his sister, almost in complaint. He was right, of course: Thalia did remember everything. All he remembered was his granduncle's garden in the backyard, and he only remembered it when, in the afternoon of the first day that they arrived, Thalia opened the battered backdoor and he followed her out into the garden. The garden, as his grandfather had told them on the way to Fresno, was his granduncle's pride. The garden was a vastness. The first thing Wesley noticed now was how it opened like an embrace taking in the drab white-brown fence, the greens drying on wires like clothes on their lines, the various yellow and red and purple vegetables that Wesley could not identify which lay in rows planted and growing out the fecund soil. Bushes and vegetables were planted along a walking path. A tree full of lemons hung over the brown fence and into the neighbor's yard, tomatoes grew out from a mass of both moist and scorched soil, and the whole sweeping vision of the yard resolved, like a crystal set in space, by the shed at its furthest, deepest edge.

The low-built shed was shelter for Frank's rottweiler. That first warm day they found the rottweiler posted just outside its shed-home. Thalia made her way straight up to it. Wesley stood by the tomatoes, a good fifty feet back from the shed and the black dog. He watched his sister now. She was with the rottweiler, in its space, on her knees, waving her hands lightly across its immense body. The shed's low ceiling threw a long black shadow over them both, so that after Thalia knelt so close it was impossible to tell one from the other.

Wesley watched the darkness. Thalia was playing games with the dog, on her hands and knees, at eye level with it, coaxing it close, then away, snaking up, letting the dog almost envelop her and then teasing it away, ending each approach. Wesley shuffled closer. The rottweiler was inches from her face. The animal was all teeth, teeth and undulating red jowls flecked with white. It had rabid eyes, red and wild that reminded Wesley of every wrung raw junkie he had ever seen. But the rottweiler was beyond human desires. Stuck-on ferocious, it moved at his sister's commands not out of love or trust but because she anticipated its instinct for violence. Wesley could see its chest and back muscles flare and expand under the skin with impossible rigor and power. He came closer. Now he was right next to Thalia.

Then the dog stood up on its hind legs, at least six feet tall. The heat and light of the day formed a watercolor warning out of the dog's black and brown fur and red and white jowls. Thalia threw out her hand like a salute and the rottweiler leapt back. His sister was obviously unafraid, but Wesley knew that if he were any more frightened, he might come out of his shoes. It wasn't just the rottweiler either, it was the heat and it was his sister and it was everything, all pressed down.

Now she was up. She dusted herself off, beckoned to him. She was beckoning him to come even closer to the dog and all of a sudden he realized the fullness of the animal's physique, the thickness through the chest, so massive; the huge jowls dripping hunger and murder; the head big like a hubcap; Wesley could hear the rottweiler's addled breathing. It was at the fence, not facing them now, but crouched low and barking and gnashing at something on the other side that. The invisible adversary barked back just as loud and shoveled up flumes of dirt that cascaded onto the rottweiler, dusting its coat like dirty rain in retaliation. The rottweiler hurled its great thickness at the fence. Wesley saw his sister flinch.

Then the shoveling stopped and the rottweiler backed away from the fence a little. Wesley sensed that somehow the two almost-warriors had called a truce. But both of them kept up with their wild, furious barking. Then Wesley's grandfather was outside with a hose, dousing the rottweiler. It bolted upright. He had to coax at the animal a little before its ears and tail fell limp and it retreated to the shed. Then Frank was outside, too. He was standing next to Thalia, watching. And Wesley stood in the spot his sister had brought him to, somewhere between his grandfather and the silenced fence, somewhere between she and the shed.

His grandfather led him back inside the house. Thalia and Frank had already gone in. His sister was in the quaint little kitchen and Frank was in the living room, standing, leaning against his old couch. Wesley felt his grandfather brush past him and into the small living room. He noted his grandfather's harsh, unnerved breathing; then its subsidence. Everything went quiet. He wandered into the kitchen, hearing the sound of his own footfalls upon the wooden floorboards. Thalia hummed something a note above silence. She reached in her back pocket and came up with a lemon. She turned on the faucet over the sink and the water tided soundlessly over the lemon and down into the convex bowl of the sink. Then she began to open and shut her granduncle's kitchen cupboards looking for a knife, and only with the wooden crashes and the metal jangling did it seem like sound reintroduced itself to the house and to his ears. Wesley looked from his grandfather to granduncle, both old men idling in the living room. He could tell they were trying to calm their nerves. "Lady ain't fixin to cut that lemon up, with me standin' here?" Frank said.

Thalia began to cut the lemon into slices.

"I could get a couple more out," she said.

"Hell she will. A lemon's just as bad as a onion or a bowel movement when it comes to its effects on a room full of people," Frank responded, his tone hot. Wesley realized his granduncle wasn't even speaking to Thalia; he was speaking to his grandfather. He never actually spoke to either him or his sister, instead choosing to direct everything at his brother, their guardian protector.

"The lemon ain't so bad," Wesley, Sr. chided. He wove his arthritic fingers round and through each other in a gesture of pain and conciliation. But he knew that being the protector of children meant starting a Civil War, brother against brother.

"If it makes me tear up, it's bad," Frank came back.

"Well, maybe you just the cryin sort. You always did have a weak constitution and as old as you are things cain't be expected to improve from here on out. Let her peel it. After all, ain't babygirl's fault you have that weak stomach."

"Old as I am!" Frank laughed, "Which of us was born first, man?"

"If you need me to remind you."

Frank sniffed. He was still leaning against his old couch but from where he could stare down the entire living room and kitchen with one put-upon expression. He said, "I've told you many times, old man, there's not too many people tougher-minded than me. I've taught high school and vocational for some twenty-six years now, and that takes a whole lot more tough than all that arts and crafts you do. Deal with the youth, see where your nerves end up. And speaking of high school, you remember Lilly, lil Lillian Jackson?"

"Ahhh, Lilly wadn't that fine in the first place," Wesley, Sr. laughed. He let himself fall down on the couch and just laughed his warmed-over laugh.

"*Not fine?*" Frank exclaimed.

"Nah, not fine. But she was something. Only lady I ever heard of went and named her daughter after herself."

"Please, man, you must'a thought she was fine. The way you were always on and on about her. You were just scared of that six-foot-seven daddy of hers. Who ended up asking her out?"

Wesley, Sr. just sighed and looked off, out the window at something.

Then the two old men plunged away on a debate about events decades dead. Wesley stopped listening to them. They argued like this a lot, over obscure and ancient matters. The boy imagined these old man arguments like light waves long since flown, probably extinguished somewhere distant, inaccessible, only now visible in their vestiges. His attention wandered with his gaze and he looked for Thalia. He saw her slipping back into the living room, back into the kitchen. She'd left the lemon face down on the kitchen countertop. And every once in a while she'd shoot a mocking, goading look at Wesley, and inch a little closer to the argument. The two old voices submerged and emerged in hyperbolic waves. After a while, they broke the surface again and the boy heard, "So not only are you laying it down that lemons are fine, but onions, too?" His granduncle waited for an answer.

There was no immediate answer.

"Well then, let me tell you why I cain't stand lady's lemon cutting. Because there ain't a lot to be happy about in Fresno these days. Streets all dirty, young people heinous, style's basically gone to hell." He paused, maybe catching his breath. "To cut a onion you need to go through each thin layer. It's hard work, doesn't seem like you gonna get no-place with it. But after enough doing you do get down to the deep parts, and you cut a lil more, lil more, looking always for that center, that seed. But you cain't see it, not here, not there. There's no center.

Life's the same way. Ain't nothing where you looking. It's all vanity. Ain't but a few things a spade can count on. And now ladygirl over there making my eyes water." He glanced over at the girl. He was smiling a kind of doing-too-much smile full of mischief. She smirked back at him. Then he said, "But she's my grandniece, not some no-relation. I guess I can find a way to live with it."

Wesley's grandfather was laughing like he was about to hack up his guts. He'd been laughing, Wesley had no idea why, from about halfway through his brother's treatise. Finally, he recovered himself enough to say. "That's your class lecture for the day. You done? Here's my lecture: For every onion there's a orange."

"Stop tryin' to sound like Confucius and shit, Negro," his granduncle said, "I got all the logic I need."

His voice was so dry, Wesley thought. Like his throat was paved with spills of hardening concrete. Thalia had long since stopped cutting the lemon into slices. She'd eaten it and now she was over with the two men, hovering back-and-forth in the space between them. His granduncle clicked his tongue against his teeth: "I've had this toothache for a while," he started in again. "This sum-bitch ain't let up, been weeks now. Gives me all these aches, be easier to tell you what don't hurt. I was thinking about a doctor visit, but he'd just root canal the thing. I ain't down with all that voodoo, people just finding ways to run away is all that is."

Wesley's grandfather shook his head and made gems with his arthritic hands.

It was strange, the feelings Wesley found birthing inside himself. He was heir to an old, violent world, older than Oakland, older than any place. Everything had melted together. Here, crystal hard, he could see again the rottweiler barking at the dog across the fence, and how his grandfather had taken a-hold of the rottweiler, subduing it somehow, and now the determined day-upon-day digging of the other dog underneath Frank's fence. One night, with the weather warm and sticky and the mist hanging in the air moist and fetid, his grandfather was cooking out on the grill in the backyard, and Wesley was there too, when the black dog appeared out of the high grass. It banged its hubcap head against his leg and for a second his knees shook in terror. He turned on the dog. It swiveled back and was staring at him open-mouthed, panting, joyful. The dog wagged its tail hopefully and Thalia's rioting laughter was an echo in the garden.

Another summer day arrived with smog hanging like rotted incense in the air. The sky was clear and endlessly blue in Oakland, where Wesley lived with his sister and grandfather. But in Fresno the sky had dressed itself with a polluted layer that in the morning could be taken for low fog but that lowered still and gritty all day long, not letting off until the evening.

Inside the house, right next to the screen door, the two kids and their granduncle mooned around thinking their separate private thoughts. They were restless but at the same time unwilling to be out in the sun too long. A little earlier, Thalia had been outside, enough engaged simply with lying in the grass, sketching a picture of the rottweiler onto a thin translucent piece of drawing paper. She lay under the lemon tree next to the metal shed and when the dog would start to slither off, she would feed it and it would remain reasonably still a little longer. The dog just stood there panting in the sun, eyes wide and tongue lolling. Even the rottweiler was surrendering to the sun. It had its metal shed to shelter under, but the dog stayed outside, idling about the garden.

Now Thalia looked as bored and removed and self-involved as the three men of the house. "Lady," their granduncle called to her, "here's a joke for you." Wesley noticed that old man's voice had nothing like the whip snap that had been in it when before he'd argued with his brother. Sleepily, the joke went on. "There's these two guys, right, being chased by a big ol bear. The first one turns to the other guy and he says, 'I don't know if we can outrun this bear.' And the other guy says, 'I don't need to outrun the bear, I just need to outrun you.'"

Their granduncle laughed. Thalia smiled. It hadn't been funny, but there was something admiring in her smile. His granduncle laughed some more about his own joke. Wesley's motiveless gaze wandered out across the smog-crusted clouds.

"What, the joke wadn't funny to you?" Thalia said.

"Nah," Wesley said.

Then Frank bent down on his creaky knees and looked through the screen door. And he was frozen there, for an instant. That surprised second was enough for Thalia and Wesley to join him kneeling and looking.

Down on the ground, almost below the ground because the hole underneath the fence was deep now, the rottweiler and the other dog were struggling against one another. Wesley could see it only in a short blur at first, just flashes of color here and there. Frank and Thalia had to wrench at the screen door just to get it to open. They went out into the yard to stop the fight. It was a minute before Wesley could join them. When he finally did and he could see what was happening, the dogs were not stopping, they were destroying vegetation, uprooting earth. The mystery dog was trying with all its might to hold position against the rottweiler, its hind legs throwing up deep earth and flowers so high he could again see the waterfall of frightened waves dying in the air and tumbling down on to both sides of the fence. The rottweiler dragged the smaller dog throat first underneath the fence into the ditch it had dug. The smaller dog let out a high shrill screech and its blood shot up like the earth and the flowers.

About an hour later, Frank Hardeman explored his garden, noting how many tomatoes had been killed off by the fight, thinking at least mine won, and wondering how it would have ended if the neighbor hadn't stepped in to save his animal. But then he remembered that it was not the tomatoes and not the dogs but finding Wesley that he was supposed to be set upon. Once Frank set back upon that goal, the resolution came fast. The boy was hiding behind the scraggly old lemon tree, silent as anything.

"Boy, is that you?" Frank called at him. Wesley flinched at the holler and didn't answer. He heard his granduncle's feet crumpling uprooted things underfoot.

"Looks like you teared up some, young buck." The old man knelt beside him where Wesley lay hid. Looking up, Wesley shook his head vehemently, not once, not twice, three times. "A'right, a'right, I can tell you were tearing up by how you deny it. Only a man would deny what's right there to see." It was a kind of compliment, actually.

Wesley could see the leaves of the lemon tree shifting in the afternoon wind.

"C'mon." Frank lifted the boy up. They went back into the house as one stricken body.

"Found him, now?" Wesley, Sr. said.

"Under the tree, by the shed," Frank said.

"Strange place for a foxhole."

"He hid good," Frank said. "Got too much pride to let us see him cry." Frank turned to Wesley, who was standing rigidly where Frank had set him on his feet by the screen door. "Pride's a good thing," his granduncle went on. "My rottweiler has it to classic degrees. I've got it, a lot of it; your sis, too." He felt Wesley's hand. "Boy, you stiff as dying. Sit down, there's no law against sitting on my couch."

Wesley went and sat on his couch.

"Good," Frank said, looking after Wesley. "Yep, I was proud of that dog for the way he got in there, you shoulda seen it, old man." They'd been so concerned with finding Wesley that the two brothers had almost forgotten the fight.

"What was there to see?" Wesley, Sr. asked, calmly, but with naked opposition in his voice too. "I mean, not to rain on your parade but all it showed is it's a dog. Dogs fight, dogs bite, they eat what they find on the ground. That fight only shows you got a dog out in that shed."

"And what's better than that?"

"I guess, maybe," Wesley, Sr. said, sudden in his weariness.

"Ah, hell." He hesitated now and looked up at his little brother wondering where his hesitation was and whether this crucible even needed to come to conclusion. Now trying to meet eyes with his brother in the garden in the moonlit night, Frank's face reminded him of the totem poles of the ancient African explorers of the Americas, those pyramidal foundations three and four thousand years old that folks said were to be found in the lands to the south of their nation along the tropic coast. Frank's great rock face was weathering on an ancient clock. There was nothing but weather and time and mystery in his face.

Frank led the rottweiler over to the far end of the yard, by the shed that shone in the moonlight. His brother followed with the gun.

"It's just a thing in life," Frank mumbled. "Old man crashed through the fence, killed that puppy unprovoked. Not that I ever seen a rottweiler fight by rules."

They were a few feet from the lemon tree, a straight line of sight from the kitchen window. The black night had gathered in full now, the kitchen light shown on the two old men like a violation, an intrusion.

"Go over to the tree," Wesley, Sr. motioned, "so the kids won't see."

"This toothache won't even let up. Not least of all for funerals," Frank said. He led the black dog over to the tree.

Inside the house, inside the hothouse kitchen where torch song light bulbs and the broiling of the stove combined to make his skin run with saltwater, Wesley divided his glances between Thalia and the half-lit backyard. He was sweating, in part, because of his sister: she, lady of the house, was preparing what she could for dinner while the two men were outside about to shoot the rottweiler. Wesley figured that as much as his sister enjoyed the huge, mean thing, she would care when it died. But she seemed unmoved. She just went about her cooking as if headed down a tunnel at the end of which was a finished meal and no sadness along the way. Thalia leaned against the kitchen sink, her back to the window and the night outside; she was ordering Wesley to get the oregano, get the knife, get this, that and everything in between.

She snapped at him, "Pick that pot up off the stove, boy, and turn the flame off while you over there." Her hair was thin-looking from all the sweat running through it. He was staring at her, not going to get anything. "Please," she added, after a moment.

He moved across the kitchen to the stove and the pot with the flame burning beneath it. He moved and the heat misted white and thick at his advance. His eyes filmed over and blurred his vision of those things not immediately before him. Outside, the sky was black. The light from the kitchen and the dark garden seemed to fuse in a haze between bright light and the dimmest vision. He couldn't even see the black dog now, just the elders. He moved across the kitchen and imagined a million ancient things where he saw only two.

"Don't be lookin out there, get the pot." Thalia was crackling with exasperation. "I'ma make dinner for you, you could least be decent, come get me that pot."

Wesley couldn't see the pistol. He knew his granduncle held it in his rough hand, poised to execute the dog. Wesley knew it was there like he knew the rottweiler was present even though its actual form had faded into blackest shadow. He knew it like he knew the sun never ceased to exist when night gathered, that it was simply behind the dark; the pistol held, poised in the night.

He was watching as his grandfather said something to his granduncle and his granduncle tapped at where his tooth ached. His granduncle's shoulders melded momentarily into a shrug. Wesley was moving through the kitchen to the stove, to the pot on the stove.

"Dang, just pick up the pot, Wesley!" Thalia cried.

His grandfather was talking at his granduncle, something about the lemon tree. His granduncle was looking down at the invisible dog, raising the invisible pistol. His arm jerked like after an injury and now both of them were staring at the invisible soil under the tree.

"And turn off the flame, like I said for you to do. Don't be lookin outside, boy!"

Wesley turned his eyes away. He determined, finally, not to look back out. He was at the stove, touching the scorching pot with his bare hands. He felt his fingers shot raw from fire as he touched it, felt something of hardness and death taken in, funneled from out of that blackness that lay crumbled beneath the lemon tree and into him, a notion of evil. And as he watched the stove flame die by his own hand and the rottweiler's nothingness fall in ultimate diminishment where the tree leaves turned, Wesley felt something extinguishing in himself. Then it had burned away completely and he knew, with anguish and with pride that his fear and his love were both diminished.

He carried the bubbling pot over to his sister, who was leaned against the kitchen sink. The pot was so hot it seemed to burn his hands deeper than the flesh. But he carried it to her and placed it on the counter beside the sink. Outside, Frank let the rottweiler slump to the ground. The destroyed carcass, less than an animal now, was difficult to look away from. It had died with its eyes staring straight at the men.

"His scratching post." Wesley, Sr. sighed. "Ah, hell."

And Frank Hardeman said something about his toothache.

❧

Wesley Sr. and the two kids went back home three days later.

Their first afternoon back, Wesley and Thalia wandered the streets and alleys rediscovering their world. East Oakland was a ghetto, of course, the gutted and foreboding shell of what, long before their birth, in a time of war and countless death, had been a model city; now just a haphazard sweep of churches and nail shops and auto repair places and Mexican and New Orleans restaurants and graffiti wall tributes to the young and the dead and a cross twenty feet high reading JESUS SAVES overlooking a prostitute stroll that stretched for miles east and west, and a sky so unadulterated blue it made the day laborers weep openly with the sunrise. The two walked up East 14th to its intersection with High Street and then up High Street not even noticing the memorial arrangement of little white crosses out front of Fremont High School.

"Ain't nothin goin on," Thalia undermined. "Wesley, you happy to be back home?"

"I don't know. Are you?"

"Nah. We was learnin out there. We seen things we won't never see here."

"Yeah," Wesley agreed. Then he looked at his sister and then he thought about all that he had seen and learned and he prayed that his eyes would never close.

ACKNOWLEDGEMENTS

My thanks and love go first and foremost to my mom and dad, Hiawatha and Calvin Norris. You are always in my heart.

Thanks also go to Crystal: *Damn, Crys!*

My writing group, thanks go to each of you: the superstar amongst us, and the two soon-to-be-uber-stars of our little literary galaxy. Also, EJ, thank you for reading some of these stories in their gestative stages.

In addition, I want to acknowledge the organizers of the 2017 Marin Headlands Fellowship and Callaloo Writers Conference (Brown University, 2016) and my teachers at UCR, Mills, and Callaloo: Susan Straight, Micheline Marcom, Victor LaValle and Ravi Howard.

Finally, I want to acknowledge two students whom I had the privilege to work with whose lives were cut short, Kimchi Truong and Terrence Meadows: may they be remembered.

KEENAN NORRIS' first novel, *Brother and the Dancer,* won the 2012 James D. Houston Award. He's completing his next novel, set in a star-crossed Oakland, and a non-fiction book about Richard Wright, Chicago, and the problem with *Chi-Raq.* He's the editor of *Street Lit: Representing the Urban Landscape* and his short work has appeared in numerous forums, including the *Los Angeles Review of Books, Oakland Noir*, popmatters.com and *BOOM: A Journal of California.*